Petr Horáček has a Master of Fine Arts degree from the Academy of Fine Art in Prague. He has been shortlisted twice for the Kate Greenaway Medal, and his books include *Song of the Wild*, *Silly Suzy Goose*, and *Puffin Peter* (all Candlewick). Born in Prague, he lives in England with his family.

Visit Petr's website at petrhoracek.co.uk or follow him on Twitter @PHoracek.

With love to Tom, Luke, and Isaac,
and everyone who cares about nature.

First published in Great Britain in 2019
by Otter-Barry Books,
Little Orchard, Burley Gate, Hereford, HR1 3QS
www.otterbarrybooks.com
Text and illustrations copyright © 2019 Petr Horáček

First published in the United States in 2020
by Eerdmans Books for Young Readers,
an imprint of Wm. B. Eerdmans Publishing Co.
Grand Rapids, Michigan

www.eerdmans.com/youngreaders

Manufactured in China.

27 26 25 24 23 22 21 20   1 2 3 4 5 6 7 8 9

ISBN 978-0-8028-5552-7

A catalog record of this book is available from the Library of Congress.

Illustrations created with mixed media.

The Last TIGER

Petr Horáček

EERDMANS BOOKS FOR YOUNG READERS

GRAND RAPIDS, MICHIGAN

Deep in the jungle
lived a fearless tiger.
No other animal was as strong
and powerful as he was.

One day hunters came to the jungle.
All the animals tried to hide.
All except the tiger.

"You have to hide!"
the other animals warned him.

"I'm not scared," growled the tiger.
"I'm the strongest, most powerful animal
in the jungle."

The next day the hunters spotted the tiger. They had never seen such a magnificent creature before.

"Catching this tiger would make us the strongest and most powerful," they thought.

The hunters returned to the city
and made a cunning plan...

Then they returned to the jungle.
There were more of them now,
and they brought nets.

Soon the tiger was overpowered and captured.

He was taken to the city
so that everyone could see him.

The tiger was kept in a cage.

People from far and wide
came to see him. They marveled
at the big, strong tiger,
as he looked out at them
from behind the bars.

He was very unhappy.

In his dreams,
the tiger ran
through the jungle.

Now, in captivity, he realized
that his strength and power meant
nothing anymore.
What he longed for was freedom.

The tiger in the cage became sadder and weaker.

Soon people stopped coming to see him.

He was getting smaller every day.

And then it happened...

One night, the tiger realized that now
he could squeeze through the bars
of his cage.

And that's exactly what he did!

The tiger walked to his freedom,
and almost nobody noticed.

In time the tiger became big and strong.
He made sure that no one would ever
see him again. And he never forgot
that his most treasured possession was
not his strength or his power...

it was his freedom.